George T. Cromwell Elementary
221 Olen Drive
Glen Burnie, MD 21061
410-222-6920

Noni Speaks Up

Heather Hartt-Sussman

Illustrated by Geneviève Côté

TUNDRA BOOKS

Tundra Books, a division of Random House of Canada Limited, a Penguin Random House Company

Library and Archives Canada Cataloguing in Publication

Hartt-Sussman, Heather, author
       Noni speaks up / by Heather Hartt-Sussman ; illustrated by Geneviève Côté.

Issued in print and electronic formats.
ISBN 978-1-77049-839-6 (bound).–ISBN 978-1-77049-840-2 (epub)

       I. Côté, Geneviève, 1964-, illustrator II. Title.

PS8615.A757N663 2016   jC813'.6   C2015-900123-4
                                                C2015-900124-2

Published simultaneously in the United States of America by Tundra Books of Northern New York, a division of Random House of Canada Limited, a Penguin Random House Company

Library of Congress Control Number: 2015931499

Edited by Sue Tate
Designed by Leah Springate
The artwork in this book was rendered digitally.
The text was set in Gotham.
Printed and bound in China

Tundra Books,
a division of Random House of Canada Limited,
a Penguin Random House Company
www.penguinrandomhouse.ca

1   2   3   4   5   20   19   18   17   16

For Mom and Dad, and for anyone who has the courage
to stand up for someone else.

– H.H.S.

For those who speak up – and those who will.

– G.C.

Noni always tries to do the right thing.
   She gives up her seat on the bus to seniors.

She holds the door open for pregnant ladies.

She even returned a bunch of loose change
to the man who dropped it at the bakery.

But, today, when she sees the kids bullying Hector at school, Noni freezes. She does not budge. She cannot get out a single word.

Noni would love to step in when the kids make fun of his name.

And his size.

And his giant glasses.

But Noni is so afraid of making enemies that she just stands there. Speechless.

When Noni was small, she didn't care who liked her.
Except her mama, of course.

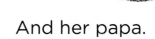

And her papa.

And the neighbor's dog, Spike. It was *really* important that she didn't make enemies with *him*.

But mostly she was happiest playing by herself.

Now Noni likes having friends, but they seem to comment on every move she makes.

"Nice *blouse*," laughs Susie when Noni shows up for a playdate.

"Gross! You're eating *that*?" says Abigail at lunchtime.

"Don't you even know how to do an *arabesque*?" says a little girl in her ballet class.

And today, when her friends announce, "We all hate Hector, don't we, Noni?" she simply does not know what to say.

Noni freezes.

She does not budge.

She cannot get out a single word.

On the way home, Noni isn't very proud of herself.

That night, Noni can't sleep. She thinks about Hector.

His name is not so terrible.
So what if he's different than the other kids?
And his glasses make him look smart!

But if Noni speaks up, her friends might turn on her.
They might call her names.
And spread rumors about her.
And trip her when she walks by.

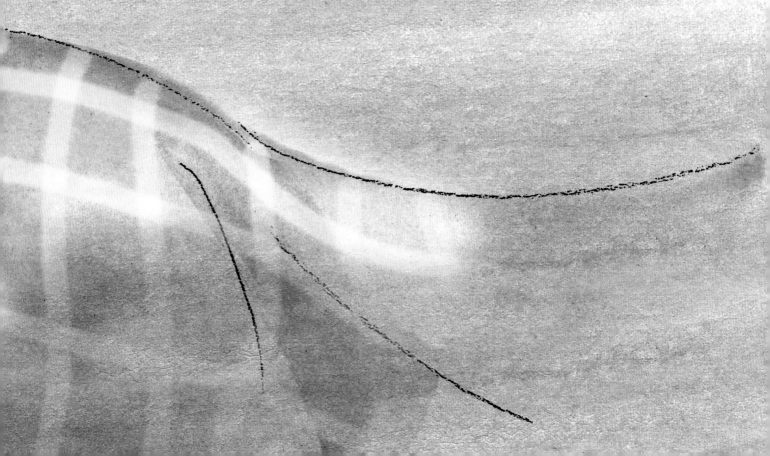

Noni imagines eating lunch alone. . . .

She pictures the kids mocking her. . . .

She sees herself having no one to play with after school. . . .

The next day, when Noni and Susie are playing in the park, Noni notices Hector on the swing.

"It's my turn!" a boy barks.

"I just got on," says Hector.

But the boy shoves him off, and Hector falls to the ground.

Noni freezes.
    She does not budge.
    She cannot get out a single word.

Meanwhile, Susie laughs. Noni can't imagine
what is funny about any of this!

Noni has had enough. It's over. Finito! Kaput!
She is done with standing by and doing nothing.
D-O-N-E. DONE!

"This is just wrong!" says Noni. "What did Hector
ever do to you?"

Susie stops laughing. Then she freezes. She does not budge. She cannot get out a single word.

"Oh, look!" mocks the boy who pushed him. "Hector needs a girl to save him."

Noni just turns to Hector and says, "Did you hear something?"

Hector smiles. With a wave of his hand, he replies, "Nah! It was nothing!"

Hector picks up his book bag. "Hey, Noni?" he says as they leave the park together. "Thanks."